DON'T TOUCH THIS BOOK!

written and illustrated by

BILL COTTER

sourcebooks
jabberwocky

Mixed media were used to prepare the full color art.

Published by Sourcebooks Jabberwocky, an imprint of Sourcebooks, Inc.
P.O. Box 4410, Naperville, Illinois 60567-4410
(630) 961-3900
Fax: (630) 961-2168
www.jabberwockykids.com

Library of Congress Cataloging-in-Publication data is on file with the publisher.

Source of Production: Leo Paper, Heshan City, Guangdong Province, China
Date of Production: June 2016
Run Number: 5006721

Printed and bound in China.
LEO 10 9 8 7 6 5 4 3 2

For Claire

Oh, hey! How's it going?

Now I know you're probably looking at my cool new book, but...

DON'T TOUCH THIS BOOK!

Don't even try it, bub.
See my picture on the front?

DON'T TOUCH THIS BOOK!

written and illustrated by **Bill Cotter**
author of DON'T PUSH THE BUTTON!

That means Larry decides who gets to play.

Tell you what...you can play, but you can only use ONE finger. Drag it. Like this.

Wow! You made blue!
Try using ALL of your fingers.

Cool! You made a rainbow!
Now try wiggling!

Yowza!
Now Spin! Spin!

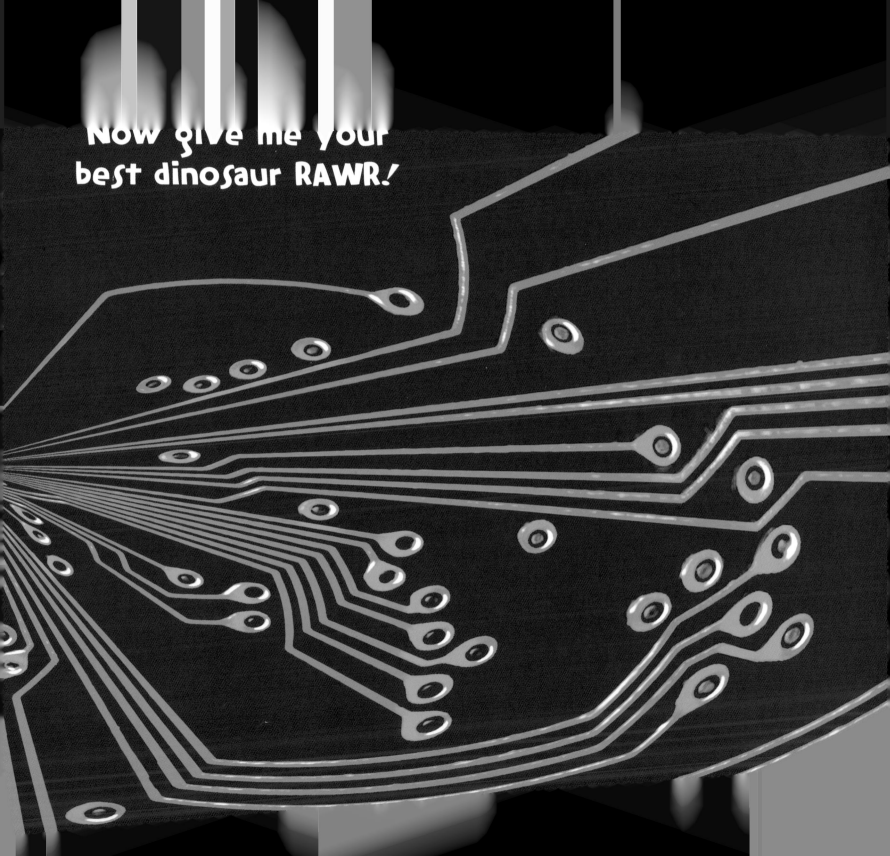

You saved me back there! That was WAY too close. We should stop. Seriously. Really.

We could try
one last thing. Let's...

WIGGLE

AND SPIN,

TALK LIKE A ROBOT,

RAWR, and

flap
our
arms

all at once...together!